Unveiled

CONFESSIONS OF A BROKEN HEART

Leyla Rodriguez

Unveiled

Copyright © 2020 Leyla Rodriguez

All rights reserved. No part of this publication may be reproduced, distributed, or transmitted in any form or by any means, including photocopying, recording, or other electronic or mechanical methods, without the prior written permission of the publisher, except in the case of brief quotations embodied in critical reviews and certain other noncommercial uses permitted by copyright law. For permission requests, write to the publisher, addressed "Attention: Permissions Coordinator," at the address below.

Any references to historical events, real people, or real places are used fictitiously. Names, characters, and places are products of the author's imagination.

ISBN: 9781094855233 (Paperback)

Written by Leyla Rodriguez

Printed by KDP in the United States of America.

First edition in 2020

Dedication

To the lovers who love to love, love, this is a piece of my soul. To the lovers who write openly without restraint, do not quit. To the lovers who came to stay without a doubt, you are loved back. To the lovers who have gone and may never return, you are not forgotten. To my friends who inspired me to be myself, who gave me a helping hand, thank you! To my acquaintances whom I have yet to get to know, you have touched my heart. To the strangers I have met along my journey, who do not know me, but I know of them, I appreciate you. To my family, who are there for me through the good times and the bad times, I love you! To my beautiful, brilliant, kind and sweet children, Miriam and Siddik, who have showed me a kind of love I didn't know existed, an unconditional kind of love, you are truly special. To all my supporters, you are the blood in my veins, my words cannot falter you, keep on loving. To my haters, you are the enemy, and I love you anyway. To the writers who are passionate and dedicated, from the past to the present, you have inspired me tremendously beyond words can ever say, continue writing. To a very special woman who is no longer here with me, my mom, who played a pivotal part in shaping my life, who showed me tough love and I will forever be grateful for it. Lastly, all this was not possible without the Divine love that has been placed inside of me for Him, and for my beloved, wherever he may be.

Table of Contents

DIVINE LOVE 1

LOST SOULS 2

SPRING 3

SHE 4

MIRROR 5

CLOSED 6

US 7

ENOUGH 8

GONE 9

VOICES 10

FORGOTTEN 11

NOSTALGIA 12

INTERNAL BEAUTY 13

JUST IMAGINE 14

A PURPOSE 15

HER 16

CHANGE THE WORLD 17

ALIVE 18

INTROVERT 19

THE GIFT OF LIFE 20

MAP OF HEART 21

I MISS YOU 22

NO REGRETS 23

FAREWELL	24
BUTTERFLIES	25
THE PEN SPEAKS	26
A SAD RHYME	27
BLEEDING NAME	28
TWO HEARTS	29
DREAMING	30
MY ADDICTION	31
ONE OF A KIND	32
PULANG	33
GOODBYE	34
LEAVE	35
HEY STRANGER	36
SECONDS	37
A SPECIAL GREETING	38
SPEAK NO MORE	39
LOVE ME AGAIN	40
MASTERPIECE	41
FREE LIKE A BIRD	42
TO LOVE OR NOT TO LOVE	43
PERFECT ARCHER	44
MOST WANTED	45
SOULMATE	46
STAY	47

AWAKE	48
FATE	49
SWEET KISS	50
TRUTH OR DARE	51
SANE WITHOUT YOU	52
JUST A WISH	53
THIS CAN'T BE LOVE	54
IT'S ME, NOT YOU	55
LOVED	56
A SILENT DEATH	57
DISGUISED	58
all he said he would	58
never do, he did. what	58
a fool I was to believe	58
a lie disguised by love.	58
COLD	59
OH, HUSBAND	60
JUST LIKE THE WIND	61
AGAINST ALL ODDS	62
ABSENT	63
THE REALITY	64
INTERVENTION	65
ONCE IN A LIFETIME	66
BURNING HEART	67

JUST ME AND YOU	68
THE END	69
PARADISE	70
SAVE ME	71
COMFORT ZONE	72
A FOOL IN LOVE	73
THE BREEZE OF THE OCEAN	74
SCALES	75
THE EDGE	76
MY SHINING STAR	77
THE STRUGGLE WITHIN	78
FAITH	79
INHALE, EXHALE	80
THE ESSENCE OF TIME	81
HUMAN KIND	82
BEYOND THE LIMITS	83
THE BEGINNING	84
AROUND THE WORLD	85
TO BE OR NOT TO BE	86
SINS	87
PASTIMES	88
BESTFRIEND	89
WITHIN ME YOU ARE	90
THE EARTH MOVED	91

TILL WE MEET AGAIN	92
INSANE	93
UNFORGIVEABLE	94
THE LESSON	95
WHAT IF	96
THE CLIMB	97
HE LOVED HER NOT	98
HIS WORD	99
AN ANGEL	100
FROM ASHES TO DUST	101
UNSPOKEN LEYLA	102
MUSIC TO MY EARS	103
SUMMER'S WIND	104
INTENTIONS	105
FORBIDDEN	106
SECRETS	107
I AM	108
THE GARDEN OF A ROSE	109
MOVING ON	110
about the author	111

DIVINE LOVE

When a girl learns that she

cannot attain her worldly

love, she yearns to reach

Divine love, the love of God.

Lianmin

LOST SOULS

Souls pass by each

other like the

seasons' wind

stroking its beauty.

SPRING

Our eyes met with a

glance of hope to

blossom like the

flowers during spring.

Lianmin

SHE

She came,

She felt,

She loved,

She left.

MIRROR

I heard you found somebody else. Every thought I never imagined to be came true. Everywhere my eyes reached flashed a picture of you in my head, in the crowd the people rushed, they pushed, and I stopped in my footsteps, pin drop silence filled the air, and there I was looking for you.

Lianmin

CLOSED

You can close your eyes to the unwanted, but you can't close your heart to the wanted.

US

I didn't know you existed.

Until I existed.

ENOUGH

He cared for her enough to leave her alone.

He cared for her enough to let her find her way—Maybe back to him.

GONE

After he left, the thoughts of him perfumed her mind more than she could ever imagine.

Lianmin

VOICES

Your voice was like thunder in my ears:

I want to get lost in your storm.

FORGOTTEN

And to thou whom

I love carelessly, you are not

forgotten by the trees, leaves

that wither away and are

reborn again— You are not

forgotten.

Lianmin

NOSTALGIA

Take me back

to the first time

we met. I want

to relive

every moment with you.

INTERNAL BEAUTY

Don't be impressed by the beauty that outlines a person. The most beautiful things are hidden.

Lianmin

JUST IMAGINE

A writer doesn't want you to read what they wrote. They want you to imagine the possibilities.

A PURPOSE

The soul is a part of your true self. It is divinely made. You cannot change the soul though you can change your actions which in turn will have an effect to the soul.

Love cannot be explained; you can try too. There are no words that can describe what you feel deep down. Only the elements of it exist. Trying to convey your feelings through words will become inevitably an attempt and others will not understand.

Life becomes worth living when you live for a purpose. There is a rebirth to a new defined you. What defines you is what you believe, your faith, your character, your personality. It all comes together to form the human being you are, the outlaying formation.

Now imagine not having a purpose to live. It raises doubt and it puts in question, the very reason of your existence. Then what are you living for?

HER

Her eyes are

the window to her

confessions: Should she let

you in?

CHANGE THE WORLD

Give the gift of love with a smile or a kind word and watch how the world changes, one person at a time.

ALIVE

How can I live like you

don't exist when you are

still alive in my heart?

INTROVERT

She notices everything about him, even the silence.

Lianmin

THE GIFT OF LIFE

When you live for something purposeful, life becomes worth living.

MAP OF HEART

The silence my heart murmurs is a tunnel leading straight to your heart.

Lianmin

I MISS YOU

I had to imagine what life would be like without you. I never imagined the pain.

NO REGRETS

Nothing is more beautiful

than two souls finding

their way towards each

other without a map, just

love.

Lianmin

FAREWELL

Bid farewell to the

love you thought you

deserved you are

worth beyond what is

hidden in the sea and

what is apparent in

the sky.

BUTTERFLIES

Her mind was

dressed in petals.

The fragrance of him

still lingers in her

heart, around her life

like a butterfly.

Lianmin

THE PEN SPEAKS

Dare to write a poem that's thought-provoking.

Hand me a pen and let my mind wander.

A SAD RHYME

It's been set in stone: your love

turned cold.

Sleepless nights of blur.

Alone again moans murmur.

Lianmin

BLEEDING NAME

We bleed the same, but we

bear different wounds,

covering the scars in solitude.

I bleed your name; an

undying sound my soul longs

to hear.

TWO HEARTS

Far in distance but so intimate in heart.

Lianmin

DREAMING

I hope that while you are asleep across the world, I am awake in your dreams.

MY ADDICTION

I thought I was addicted to sushi but then you came along, and you smiled. After that, my world has been in total chaos.

Lianmin

ONE OF A KIND

You know that kind of love the

one you compare to others it's

a one of a kind of love you felt

it once and you don't want to

feel no other how sad it is to

lose that kind of love

it still lives

inside of you

it breathes moments of

passion

will I ever let go and love

another kind of love?

PULANG

The abduction from your love has awakened in the darkest of nights, even a dead soul.

She waited for him to return, thoughts racing back and forth through her mind. Does he still love her? Has he given up so easily?

Maybe a text or bouquet of flowers could rekindle an old flame.

GOODBYE

I wanted to forget:

November, undated, fear

of loss as I held your frail

hands unto mine

till your last breath; a silent

goodbye, a teardrop.

LEAVE

Either stay and be forgiving or leave.

Leave me to fend for my kind, the kind

you ruined like a tragedy again and

again— I am not the same.

Lianmin

HEY STRANGER

Come, come whoever you are:

traveler, lover of leaving

unfamiliar souls who have

embarked on a lost journey.

Come, stay whoever you are:

lover.

SECONDS

My love, don't leave

me for one second. I

might lose myself.

Lianmin

A SPECIAL GREETING

I send my greetings to the lovers who have been broken. Somehow, they manage to smile while every bone in their body is completely numb.

SPEAK NO MORE

For the first time, my pen has been lifted, the ink has dried, and my words have died.

Lianmin

LOVE ME AGAIN

Meet me where we first met in

the lovers' lane riding the

Ferris wheel.

Do you remember almost

touching the sky, captivated by

the stare

in your eye? I cried in agony

when I felt the butterflies in my

stomach flutter away how lovers

do

when they

fall out of love.

MASTERPIECE

Hopelessly loving the

voices of your hidden love,

even the silence between

two souls. Yearning for

what could have been

a masterpiece of you and

me.

Lianmin

FREE LIKE A BIRD

Could it be that you feel my pain? My soul has suffered enough from this love.

Release me like a bird to the skies that do not judge.

TO LOVE OR NOT TO LOVE

To thou I made a promise to love or not to love. I chose love by your hand and by your heart. I kept my pity to myself, then tried to let the pain fade away into the shadows of myself. Without this love, I cannot love.

Lianmin

PERFECT ARCHER

Your words are like arrows aiming

at my heart ready for war.

MOST WANTED

You made my heart your home, and I'm waiting for your return. This time promise me to stay where you belong: the lost and found.

Lianmin

SOULMATE

Maybe we lived a
thousand lives before
this one, before we met,
and in each one, we keep
finding each other.

STAY

It was his eyes on the prowl that
could never look away, seeking
from her what she seeks from him.

A word or two
felt like déjà vu.

Come hither and stay for a
while— maybe forever.

Lianmin

AWAKE

My dreams and nightmares

are the same with or

without you.

FATE

No one will make you feel wanted more than destiny.

Lianmin

SWEET KISS

What comes from the heart truly belongs to the heart, even if it's a kiss goodnight through the phone.

TRUTH OR DARE

You can convince yourself that the truth doesn't exist, but who will convince God?

Lianmin

SANE WITHOUT YOU

The only problem with loving someone is that it might make you insane.

JUST A WISH

I'm exhausted from
loving you. Let me live
in my dreams where
you love me too.

Lianmin

THIS CAN'T BE LOVE

Without you I am no more than

a living heart beating, trying to

exist in the world. I just want to

escape from my very own soul.

I'll risk everything and

anything to be with you,

even if you don't love me.

IT'S ME, NOT YOU

She is most beautiful in

the wee early morning

hours before sunrise

without makeup,

without filters— when

she first opens her eyes

and sees you.

Lianmin

LOVED

If only I existed in his heart how he exists in mine. Oh, how lovely that would feel: To love and to be loved by the only one you wish to love.

A SILENT DEATH

I love the silence

between two lovers craving the

attention, yearning for the

company,

wishing she could hear your

thoughts about her.

Quietly in despair of each

other.

Oh, the agony must be

killing him.

Lianmin

DISGUISED

all he said he would

never do, he did. what

a fool I was to believe

a lie disguised by love.

COLD

The tears roll down my face one

drop at a time as if you could see

the transparency of my pain slowly

showing itself on me.

Your distant, I'm

cold and lonely,

emotionally

deprived of what

was once alive;

what was once

called love still

haunts me, and

here I am still

wanting you,

waiting.

Lianmin

OH, HUSBAND

I still look for you, I still compare us.

Somewhere in the far corners of the world, in him and in her as a part of me and my heart continues beating for what we had beautifully built within each other's soul.

JUST LIKE THE WIND

...and just as the air cannot

be seen but breathed,

we ceased to exist

as an unpleasant

memory of a dying love.

Lianmin

AGAINST ALL ODDS

What does it take

to love when the body feels

compelled to do so against

the odds of loving?

ABSENT

Meet me where

the stars touch the moon

When I'm gazing off into the

far stretches of the night, I

long for your voice, I long for

your smile, two souls

intertwined as one body, one

heart return at once for I can

no longer bear the absence

of my beloved.

Lianmin

THE REALITY

It felt like a dream, you

are loving me and me

loving you

until I finally

opened my eyes reality

sunk in.

I'm in more pain now and

I can't stop crying.

INTERVENTION

Tell me is there any love

more beautiful than the one

true God has placed

inside me for you?

Lianmin

ONCE IN A LIFETIME

So many times

I wanted to utter

I love you I waited,

hoping for the

perfect

moment maybe

you will feel the

same one day.

BURNING HEART

He was the one

I never saw coming

who ignited my heart to

flames beyond my control.

Lianmin

JUST ME AND YOU

I wish I could freeze

time when you said I

love you, so that I could

live in that moment

forever.

THE END

I stood there helpless in silence

as he ripped a piece of my

heart out in front of my eyes

while confessing his love for me

should I stay a little while

longer till the torments of my

mind, body and soul cease to

your needs or do I walk away

now avoiding the unfathomable

end of me and you.

Lianmin

PARADISE

This world is where life

begins and the

hereafter is where love

never ends.

SAVE ME

He came

like a hurricane,

washed away some of

my pain and now I'm drowning

in his love.

COMFORT ZONE

In the absolute still of the night, where there is no sound and there is no movement. There is only the beating of your heart, I can feel throbbing against my chest, it has become a part of me. It moves my soul from one place to another without force. Maybe it was love that had me choked up, not able to speak, leaving me alone, and desperate for your presence. Maybe it was because I was comfortable being close to you, almost paralyzing me. I no longer cared to be.

A FOOL IN LOVE

Your love makes me
feel like a fool easy to
fall for but hard to
catch.

Lianmin

THE BREEZE OF THE OCEAN

When you close your eyes look

for me by the sea where the

waves brush through the winds

the sound of my love crashing

against the ripping tides

I'm there waiting to see

you again.

SCALES

Love is a balance

You keep me sane

I'll make you crazy.

Lianmin

THE EDGE

He kept pushing her love to the edge, to the point of no return.

MY SHINING STAR

Will he ever

understand he is the

only star in my galaxy

I love gazing at.

Lianmin

THE STRUGGLE WITHIN

Why do we have to go through this? No, I am not asking why the Lord allows this to happen. I'm responsible for my actions which are the direct result of the consequences, I dare to face in this world and in the next. What will be waiting for me in the hereafter if I don't go through what I have been fighting for? I can't fight against my fate, against the will of God. I am only fooling myself, tricking myself into believing I can go on like this.

FAITH

Believe you are destined for greatness.

Not because of who you are, but because of the Divine One who created you.

Lianmin

INHALE, EXHALE

I tried to open myself to
the possibilities of love,
loving you, without fear
without regrets, and I
can't.
It still lives
inside of me inhaling,
breathing into the
past, exhaling into the
future, into the
existence of who I
am— and who I have
become.

THE ESSENCE OF TIME

Give love the time it needs

the condiments to grow

the space to explore the

chance to survive in this

harsh world I'm giving you

time to breed a beautiful

creation with me.

Lianmin

HUMAN KIND

Sometimes the voice you need to hear is found in others.

Sometimes the words you need to say is written by someone else.

We live like strangers amongst each other, but we are no different.

BEYOND THE LIMITS

Is there such thing as to

love too deep beyond

the core of my heart's

limitations?

Blinded by love

and everything that

consumes you breathes

inside of me.

THE BEGINNING

He said I love you first. What did it signify? What did it transpire? I thought it was the beginning of a never-ending love story. I said I love you too. Why did I let my guard down, my vulnerability shattered to pieces. Was is it because of the eloquent words we do not hear so often? Then, why start believing in words that cannot be defended? It's just that, I wanted to believe everything he said, and I did, even the red flags. Though his every word seemed like a dream, faltered. I stood there taking the punches with every blow straight to the heart, instead of running away. I knew the truth, he confessed in his own tongue. Maybe it was too late, I was already sold on fake promises, false pretentious feelings were my weakness, I fell prey so easily. He never cared. Not once did his words proved to be true. I finally understood that only God knows the truth.

AROUND THE WORLD

If I could meet you anywhere in the world, I would meet you halfway, where your heart finds my soul.

Lianmin

TO BE OR NOT TO BE

Have you ever gotten that feeling of nostalgia? Like the spoken word had come alive and you are the living proof. You had been there before or maybe you wished you had. It's a strong connection, a blissful feeling, mixed emotions, a fleeting of rage released by the soothing sound of her voice. You know her from somewhere but nowhere. You don't know how to react, or what to say, love has claimed its location without your consent. Fate has determined what was meant to be will be, even if we never met before. This is the Divine calling between souls created before being born. Wherever you reside my beloved, may your name be written next to mine.

SINS

Yes rain

on me with your

divinity;

my unwanted

sins need

cleansing.

Lianmin

PASTIMES

We try to let go of the past, yet the past has a way of following us into the future, and wherever we go. We live with the burden upon our shoulders. We keep asserting ourselves that life goes on, new memories will be reborn, beautiful people will come across our path again. The sadness of a heavy heart, and the pain from the past, with engorged wounds that are sealed, we accept them as they are and one day, we lose them. Woe to love.

BESTFRIEND

It doesn't matter how much time seemed to pass by or how many seasons shifted from morning to night, it is you I still want. The dilemma about that is, I know you don't want me. Though, I could never tell, from the beginning it was a magical connection, from the laughs to the late-night tales, to the not so memorable moments, we bonded instantly. I couldn't hang up the phone, I didn't want to, I wanted to know more about you, not really, I just wanted to hear your voice. The subject of our conversations was a joke sometimes. I could talk to you about the birds and the bees, about how blue the sky looked that day, what about the cheese, as long as you listened, the sky was the limit. That is what I miss, what my heart yearns for, someone who I thought would still be there for me somewhere on the sidelines cheering me on.

Lianmin

WITHIN ME YOU ARE

I stood quiet for too long but the voices inside of me never stopped talking. Why should I have to tell you what to do, or how to treat a woman, maybe I should come with a manual next time.

I gave signals hoping you would catch on to the very least by showing me some type of love. Didn't you want to spend time with me, I would often ask myself. It didn't have to be diamonds or a date to a fancy restaurant, it could've been just you and me, anywhere and anytime, looking into each other's eyes. The stars and moon would be jealous, though they still shine at night because they exist within each other. You were always that for me.

THE EARTH MOVED

When I fell asleep,

I wished this was a

dream to only wake up

to your silence instead

of to the sound of your

voice playing in my ear.

Remember when you

laughed so hard, I swear

the earth shifted its axle a

little from your happiness.

If only we were happy

together, I'm sure even

the angels would have

rejoiced, and the world

would smile.

Lianmin

TILL WE MEET AGAIN

You are somewhere across the world asleep, and here I am awake because your love won't let me rest. As if the two souls have already intertwined becoming one. Yet the souls have separated into their own world, to a path unknown. What has become of me without you, my beloved? How could we let this happen without putting up a fight? It was a fatal goodbye, harsh words of a dying love never meant for me.

INSANE

I will be honest with you; I didn't understand his crazy mind. All I knew was that he loved me with every bit of his wild madness, even his family couldn't tame. I accepted him for who he was, I believed in us when the world opposed us. Gosh, you made me cry when you sang a lullaby, a song made for me and you. You could feel my sadness from thousands of miles away, I always wondered how. It was the love you knew. We used to send heartfelt messages I could feel, and you could translate. In the end, you lost your mind. I tried searching for you before your love started to fade away into a once upon a time memory. I held on as long as I could, insanity took over your mind and killed our love.

Lianmin

UNFORGIVEABLE

If I could do it all over again, I would, just to hear you say you love me one more time. I believe we get used to the pain after a while, we learn to live with the wounds which at one point almost felt unbearable, the delicate sensitive scars we are afraid of looking at, of touching. Then you say I should love again, when I haven't even healed yet. Will I ever heal? Will the scars somehow blend into my skin forming a smooth surface. Will I love again, the way I loved you? I don't want to love anybody else. You are a part of me no one can take away. Don't tell me to love again.

THE LESSON

The pain you have gained becomes a blessing, in it there are lessons waiting to be learned. Until we can accept the pain as it entered us, we must understand that perhaps we need to change. It is Divine intervention planning, as we are busy pondering while we are planning. We oftentimes, tend to overlook beyond the repairs of a broken heart. Let go of the pain and let God do the rest, so you can finally be at peace.

Lianmin

WHAT IF

I keep asking what if, even after the storm has destroyed everything, even after it has passed. What if you were here with me now, would my life be any different? What if, we didn't break up, would I be any happier? What if, I could speak to you right now, would it change your mind about your love for me?

What has become our fate, the separation of me and you, are the truth. The reality of what if has become our fate, and yet I am still hoping and wondering about you, about us, about our love. When will what if become a reality to me? As if the pain I have endured isn't enough already living without you. I keep whispering to myself, what if you weren't the one who got away.

THE CLIMB

I would climb over mountains to see your face again, my ears would fall deaf to the sound of someone else's voice other than yours, my eyes would look for you in the crowd for I have eyes only for you, and when the world is asleep, I'm hoping you are seeking me too.

Lianmin

HE LOVED HER NOT

He loved her not for the rosy cheeks she had when he made her smile or when he looked her way.

He loved her not for the brightest days or the darkest nights they shared.

He loved her not for everything that felt right but were wrong.

He loved her not for everything that was wrong but felt so right.

He loved her not for the beauty she radiantly wore which always ignited his heart. For the sake of God alone, he loved her endlessly. Isn't that enough?

HIS WORD

I remember his words faintly they still resonate with me every day, he said "I love you for everything that you are not what you promise to be. I know you can't see why or how you're the most important person to me." Where are you now?

Lianmin

AN ANGEL

He asked her where she comes from. He wanted to taste her darkness, wanted to sip every rain drop from her skin, she is so beautiful, if only you could see what I saw. He promised, before every sunrise and in every moon's shed, to never leave. He didn't want to lose her, she is like no one you have ever seen, did she come from heaven or is she an angel in the form of a human soul.

FROM ASHES TO DUST

Your eyes have

burned a hole in

my heart scatter

my body

like sand into the

ocean over the

moon's shadow

and

let me sink.

UNSPOKEN LEYLA

My imaginary words

spoke nothing but

sentiments of a broken

heart.

MUSIC TO MY EARS

He sang a song to the
melodies of my heart.

My body's rhythm
and soul has
completely fallen in
tune with his.

Lianmin

SUMMER'S WIND

I'll risk my life to have one more chance with you.

I'll risk everything to have you next to me.

So close, almost caressing my face with your scent. Yet so far, like the summer's wind that blows away in the nights dusk and never returns.

And then he was, he became, all I ever imagined to be. Mine.

INTENTIONS

Love the unforgivable.

They make mistakes too.

Lianmin

FORBIDDEN

What has become of us, in only three days, by the faint distance that captured our hearts, surely it felt like a lifetime of memories well kept. What will become of us if you are not mine, and I am not yours? Can we depart amicably without the thorn of the roses? The fall of the rain turned my sunshine into clouds, you still found me wavering the fohn, even if you are not like me, casted out from the others, intensely we merged beautifully into one faith called love.

SECRETS

Sometimes we hide the pain in shame; we live with our secrets which have shaped our future.

I AM

Do not love me for who

I am, for I am no one as

love transforms who

you are, then you

should be free to love.

THE GARDEN OF A ROSE

I smelled the sweet rose from

the garden its scent lingered

traveling through my nose

grazing every part of my skin,

passing through my veins even

after I was gone it opened my

heart to its beautiful fragrance

and to the surroundings of life.

In that moment a deep sense

of melancholy and longing filled

the atmosphere, it was you.

Lianmin

MOVING ON

Is there really no one like me, I thought

countless of times. Was it because of the way

he treated me, I allowed too often.

If I could just tell you one thing

I'd say give us a chance again.

I asked for a little sympathy for us.

We were young, falling for mistakes.

I couldn't stop myself from leaving

after you shattered our dreams. My every being tried

to forget and accept the deceit of you. only to discover

it wasn't worth the grief.

about the author

Leyla Rodriguez is a poet by heart who loves to love love, additionally over the years she has developed a passion for writing stories for children. Besides writing she is an entrepreneur, who is spiritually in sync with her religion. When she is not busy exploring the blank pages, she gets lost somewhere into the magical world creating unforgettable memories with her two beautiful children. You can learn more about upcoming projects by visiting her website http://unspokenleyla.com/.

Made in United States
North Haven, CT
11 February 2024